THE GHOST BUTTERFLY

Story by
Adam Cornish

Illustrated by
Rachel Batislaong

ISBN: 978-1-9999688-9-2

Edited by E. Rachael Hardcastle
Formatted by E. Rachael Hardcastle
Written by Adam Cornish
Illustrated by Rachel Batislaong

Published by Curious Cat Books, United Kingdom
For further information: www.curiouscatbooks.co.uk

Also available as an e-book.
1st Edition

"For Mum and Dad.
Without your fibs, this wouldn't exist."

Walls and ceilings, I glance off,
I flap, float and zoom!

A spooky wee beastie,
the pest in your room.

With wings snowy grey, speckled with brown,
my manoeuvres are so swift,
you will **never** pin me down.

Everybody panics when I flutter by.
And rightly they should, I'm a ghost butterfly!

I'll **tap** on your lamp,
because the light I like low.

I'll **bump** against your TV,
when I don't like the show.

When you open the drawer,
where you keep your socks,
I'll **spring** out towards you,
to give you a shock.

OoO**O**!

It's a lonely life for me,
when people tell me to "**shooooo!**"

But I'm a **ghost butterfly,**
and scaring folk is what I do.

Then on one summer's day,
I was watching you play,
with your toys and all your friends,
and wished I could do the same.

If I could be less creepy,
when all is said and done,
maybe we'd be pals,
and I could join in the fun?

I must make an effort,
my ways I must mend,
because I'm always so alone,
it would be better with friends.

Starting from now,
a nice guy I'll be.

When you're naming your friends,
on that list will be me.

You don't have to worry,
scaring is no longer my style.

So now when you see me,
you won't **shriek**, you'll smile.

When you get home,
I'll be the first to say **hi**.

I prefer it this way,
as our friendship now thrives.

Even your dog woofs **hello**,
and the cat gives me **high fives**.

At the end of the day,
being spooky was fun.

Yet, life is much sweeter,
with you as my chum.

I may still look **eerie**, be don't be put off.
I'm a **ghost butterfly**...

But most call me **Moth!**

Lightning Source UK Ltd.
Milton Keynes UK
UKHW050317241220
375536UK00009B/29